CATHEDRAL MOUSE

CATHEDRAL MOUSE

KAY CHORAO

E. P. DUTTON · NEW YORK

Copyright © 1988 by Kay Sproat Chorao
Published in the United States by E. P. Dutton,
2 Park Avenue, New York, N.Y. 10016,
a division of NAL Penguin Inc.

Published simultaneously in Canada by
Fitzhenry & Whiteside Limited, Toronto

Editor: Ann Durell   Designer: Riki Levinson

Printed in Hong Kong by South China Printing Co.
First Edition   W   10 9 8 7 6 5 4 3 2 1

Library of Congress Cataloging-in-Publication Data
Chorao, Kay.
    Cathedral mouse / by Kay Chorao.—1st ed.
        p.   cm.
    Summary: Little Mouse is befriended by a stone carver at a cathedral.
    ISBN 0-525-44400-9
    [1. Mice—Fiction.   2. Cathedrals—Fiction.
    3. Stone carvers—Fiction.]   I. Title.   87-33398
PZ7.C4463Cat   1988   CIP
[E]—dc 19   AC

to Kristin, who planted the seed
that grew into the idea for this book

rom the day Mouse was born, he wanted a home. A real home.

Mouse was so small, no one saw him slip out of the pet store onto the snowy street.

No one saw him sniff the stalks of sugarcane and crates of fruit outside the bodega.

But in front of the meat market someone did see him. The big orange cat who worked there.

Mouse ran for his life across the street, up some broad stone steps, and through a towering doorway.

He found himself in a vast space, dim and echoing with mysterious sounds.

Mouse was in a cathedral.

Near him, candles flickered on a low polished table. Mouse curled up near the golden lights to warm himself. But a hand came toward him and Mouse felt danger, so he ran again.

He dashed past human feet, up a carved screen, higher and higher until he came to rest, his heart pounding.

He darted in and out of the windows and doors, in and out, up and down.

But faces loomed out of the shadows and frowned at him.

Mouse leaped from the screen and scurried for safety.

As he ran, he caught a scent.

"Mice," he whispered, "mice!"

Mouse scampered along a railing, up a wall and, slipping and sliding, fell tail first down a long, long organ pipe.

Thump!

At the bottom of the pipe, Mouse tumbled into a nest of mice.

"Out! Get out! You are not one of ussssssss," they hissed.

They were large and gray. Mouse was small and spotted.

"But . . ." said Mouse.

"OUT," they said, rising like a fierce gray wall.

Mouse ran out through a hole in the organ pipe and fell head over heels into the choir stall. He ran along the top and leaped over the edge. He landed on the head of a carved lamb and slid down its nose into a cozy hollow.

Mouse hid there, his heart still thumping.

No one came. It was quiet. So Mouse curled his tail over his nose and snuggled down.

Then . . . *crash!*

A large hymnbook fell through the air and narrowly missed him.

Mouse dashed away, running, running to find a safe place.

Finally he reached the top of a stone pillar.

"I will sleep here tonight. And tomorrow I will find a home."

So Mouse fell asleep, cold and alone.

In the morning, he was awakened by a delicious smell. Next to him lay some bread and cheese.

He ate them hungrily. And while he ate, he peered out at the world around him.

Light fell jewel-bright through windows. Pale ribbons of light cut through the endless space. Beams of light made soft, glowing patterns on the marble floor.

Mouse scampered down his pillar.

"Blue mouse toes. Red mouse tail," he sang, dancing in the light.

But suddenly a huge mop crashed down, almost crushing him. A man shouted, and Mouse ran back to his pillar.

"I must learn to be more careful," Mouse said. And he did.

He learned to explore and slide and sing and play when everything felt safe and quiet. At other times, he slept on his pillar.

Sometimes when he awakened, more bread and cheese were beside him.

"This pillar is safe, and it gives me bread and cheese," said Mouse, "but it is still not a real home."

One day Mouse almost dashed against the shoe of a man.

The man was standing in the shadows near the pillar.

"Ah, there you are," said the man.

Mouse froze with fear.

But the man's voice was soft and slow. "Don't be afraid," he said, reaching his hand toward Mouse.

Mouse did not move. He looked at the man, and the man looked at him and smiled. Slowly the man moved his hand closer. Mouse leaped to his pillar and scrambled to the top. The man walked away, nodding his head and smiling to himself.

After that, the man came often. Each time, he reached out his hand. And each time, Mouse let it come a little closer, until at last the man touched Mouse's head.

Then one day Mouse felt brave enough to step onto the man's hand—for just a moment.

And after a very long time, Mouse let the man lift him up and give him rides high on his arm.

Then, finally, Mouse let the man slip him into his pocket. In the pocket Mouse found a surprise. Bread and cheese! They tasted just like the bread and cheese on Mouse's pillar.

The man laughed when Mouse popped his head out of the pocket, his furry cheeks stuffed with his favorite food.

"Tomorrow I will take you to my workshop so you can keep me company, little Cathedral Mouse," said the man.

And so he did.

The man gently tucked Mouse into the cuff of his woolen cap, where Mouse could stay warm but see everything. Together they went through a side door of the cathedral. Then they went into a shed filled with blocks of stone.

The man took off his cap and placed it on a stool.

"Now, my little friend, you can curl up in my cap and watch," said the man.

So Mouse watched from his woolly perch. He watched the man pound stone with a large wooden hammer. He pounded and pounded against a nail-like tool. All the pounding made a white dust from the stone. By the end of the day, the man was covered with white dust like powdered sugar.

After that, the man often took Mouse to his workshop. On other days, Mouse slid and sang and danced and played in the cathedral.

But at the end of every day, Mouse returned to his pillar.

"It is not a real home, but it is safe," said Mouse.

Then one day he could not return. A group of men were pushing something heavy onto the top of his pillar.

"Now I have no place at all," said Mouse.

He slowly left his high perch and sadly passed by his pillar.

But a big, warm hand reached out and lifted him up.

"Look what I have carved for you," said Mouse's friend.

Mouse looked.

"You have carved . . . ME!" said Mouse.

"And more," said the man. He set Mouse gently on the stone.

Mouse crept into a tunnel, just his size, and found a cozy little room.

"A home," said Mouse. "Now I have a real home."

"And now you are a real Cathedral Mouse," said the man.

And so he was, and so he would always be, forever and ever.